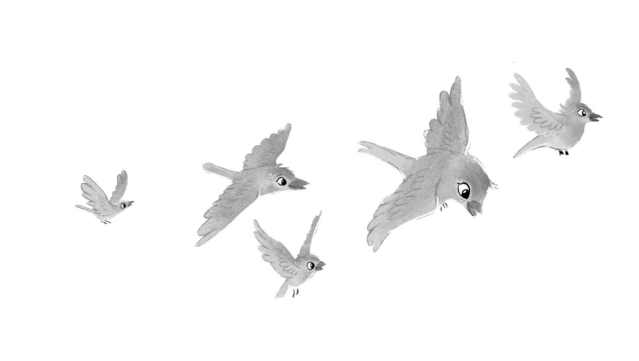

Dear Reader:

The death of a loved one means changes in your child's life accompanied by worries and fears about what happens next.

Grief is a process. The way children cope with loss depends largely on how they are supported through their loss. Encourage them to put their emotions into words. Big emotions like anger, sadness, and fear are common in grieving hearts.

The bluebird carries the universal symbol of joy and happiness and has become an emblem of hope for my family after we lost my mom to cancer.

Shortly after the funeral, my family started making bluebird houses in my mother's memory, needing one last connection to her. The bluebird was her favorite bird. She loved the sky-blue coloring on its back and the earth-brown coloring on its chest, representing love transcending from the heavens to our loved ones on earth. What started as a way to work through grief has turned into the heart-forward business of building homes for the bluebird of happiness and giving back with proceeds from each exchange.

You can find our family at "Rudolph's Bluebird Houses" on Facebook. We ship throughout the US through the shop section of our page.

I hope that the message in *Rise Up, Little Bluebirds* can aid your grief process. It's not so isolating when we help each other through it.

ISBN: 978-1-63489-458-6
Library of Congress Catalog Number has been applied for.
Printed in the United States of America
First Printing: 2021

25 24 23 22 21   1 2 3 4 5

Written by Kristy Boike
riseuplittlebluebirds.com

Illustration by Kathryn Inkson
kathryn-inkson.co.uk

Design by Aurora Whittet Best
redorganic.com

WISE
INK

807 Broadway Street NE, Suite 46
Minneapolis, MN 55413
wiseink.com

RISE UP,
LITTLE BLUEBIRDS

written by **Kristy Boike** *and illustrated by* **Kathryn Inkson**

*Dedicated to my four little bluebirds: Matthew, Grace, Ryan, and Noah;
and to my father, who taught me the meaning of strength*

Rise up, little bluebirds,
it's time to start the day.
There is so much to share
since Grandma Bluebird passed away.

When Grandma Bluebird left this world,
the world felt sad and blue.
Grandma's heart held a special love
for every one of you.

That love lives on inside you now, even though she's gone.
Her love fills every breakfast, every game, and every song.

Rise up, little bluebirds,
find strength to spread your wings.
It's time to see all the beauty
that Grandma's love still brings.

She couldn't wait to see you brave
and ready at the door.

She would be proud
you've grown up ready
to conquer more.

She loved the blooming flowers
in the meadows far and wide.
Whenever you fly near them,
feel her love right by your side.

In the meadow, Mole helped Grandma
choose her favorite blooms.

She had a new bouquet they picked in every single room.

Mole has been feeling sad
since Grandma Bluebird died.
She hasn't picked the flowers
she used to bring inside.

Let's help Mole choose flowers
that Grandma would have loved.
The forget-me-nots and goldenrod
carry her love from up above.

Grandma Bluebird loved the prairie,
where she picked berries to eat.
Her friend Hare baked pies
with those berries and golden wheat.

Look! Friend Hare is busy in the
kitchen, baking perfect berry pies.
Keeping her hands busy
helps her feel less alone since
Grandma died.

But then Hare slams the oven door shut,
angry she's by herself.
Instead of giving pies to Grandma,
extra pies go on her shelf.

Let's stop in and see
if Hare could use a friend.

It's important to cheer her up before our visit ends.

The bridge across the pond
was Grandma's favorite spot to rest.
Remember how she always gathered
the softest branches for her nest?

She used the leftover branches
to make art with her friend Loon.

They loved to paint pictures together
underneath the rising moon.

Loon's too sad to paint anymore,
because it only makes her cry.
But having an outlet for your grief
can help the days go by.

The world can feel empty and sad
when someone close to us dies.
It's a big change in our lives,
and big emotions can arise.

When we think of her,
it's okay to feel **sadness**, **anger**, and **fear**.
It helps to remember how Grandma
still touches everyone she held dear.

We'll have a potluck
tonight with Grandma
Bluebird's family
and friends.

Sharing her life with those who knew her
ensures her love will never end.

Your older siblings, aunts, uncles, and cousins
will meet us in the meadow.
We'll grieve together with all her neighbors
underneath the weeping willow.

You don't have to be with Grandma Bluebird
to feel her love go all around.
Her love is in every smile,
every story, and every sound.

Friend Mole can bring beautiful flowers,
friend Hare can bring some pie.
Friend Loon can bring her art,
even though it made her cry.

Everyone grieves differently,
and there are lots of good ways to cope.
Helping those you love through sadness
is what can give us hope.

Rise up, little bluebirds, when you see someone in need. There are still flowers to pick, art to make, and mouths to feed.

Those are all the little things in life
that Grandma Bluebird loved the best.
It's all those little things we still enjoy
that make us feel loved and blessed.

Rise up, little bluebirds,
and know that although we are apart,

Grandma Bluebird is gone from our nests,

but she'll **never** leave our hearts.

Kristy Boike is a mother of four from Minnesota with a background in early childhood education. She lives with her husband and four children, who struggled through the loss of her mom to cancer in early 2018. Shortly after the loss of her mother, she lost her father-in-law to cancer as well. Seeing the way those losses affected her children made her want to create a way to guide them through grief. After her family's success with Rudolph's Bluebird Houses, she became passionate about giving hope to people big and small who have lost, or are anticipating the loss of, a loved one. Kristy is available for workshops and speaking engagements.

Kathryn Inkson is an illustrator from northeast England who celebrates animals and natural themes in her artwork. When she's not illustrating, she loves going on long countryside walks with her dog Primrose, riding horses, and reading fairy tales.

To learn more about Kristy's work
around grief and healing, go to
riseuplittlebluebirds.com